First published in the United States, Great Britain, Canada, Australia, and New Zealand
in 2009 by North-South Books Inc., an imprint of NordSüd Verlag AG, CH-8005 Zürich, Switzerland.
Distributed in the United States by North-South Books Inc., New York 10001.

Library of Congress Cataloging-in-Publication Data is available.
ISBN: 978-0-7358-2265-8 (trade edition).
10 9 8 7 6 5 4 3 2 1
Printed in Belgium

www.northsouth.com

The GIFTS

BY REGINA FACKELMAYER
ILLUSTRATED BY CHRISTA UNZNER

NorthSouth
New York / London

It was Christmas Eve. Mia stood in the marketplace and looked into her shopping basket. "Now let's see," she said to herself. "A turkey for Christmas dinner, a chewy bone for Murphy, a catnip mouse for Mopp, a new winter hat for me, some decorations for the tree—Oh! I almost forgot the tree!"

Mia hurried off to the Christmas tree lot.
She picked out a lovely little tree in a pot.

On her way home, it started to snow. The ground was getting very slippery. Suddenly an old man right in front of her slipped on the icy ground.

Down he fell. His packages scattered all around him. Mia hurried to help him up.

"Thank you," said the old man.

"You're welcome," said Mia. "Here, let me help you pick up your presents."

In no time at all, the man's presents were all back in his sack.

Mia waved good-bye. "Merry Christmas!" she called.

When she got home, Murphy and Mopp were there to
greet her. "Get your nose out of my basket, Mopp!" Mia laughed.
But when she began to unpack, she remembered the tree.

"Oh, no!" she cried. "I must have forgotten it when I helped the old man. Murphy, fetch a broom. We're going to find our Christmas tree!"

Mia put on her new Christmas hat, and she and Murphy set out.

Mia and Murphy kept on looking. They found a garbage can and a mailbox, but no Christmas tree.

"There it is," Mia cried, "covered with snow!" But when she and Murphy brushed the snow away, there was a fire hydrant, not a Christmas tree.

It was getting dark, so Mia and Murphy headed sadly for home.
Right in front of their house, they met a little boy. He was crying.
"Are you looking for your Christmas tree too?" Mia asked.
"No." The boy sniffled. "I lost my hat when I was sledding, and
my grandpa is going to be very angry."

"You're going to catch cold without a hat," said Mia.

"Here, take mine and run home quickly. It's Christmas Eve!"

"Oh, thank you!" said the little boy.

"Merry Christmas!" Mia called after him.

Mia flopped down into her favorite chair and sighed.
"Christmas without a Christmas tree isn't quite the same."
Suddenly Murphy jumped up and ran to the door.

There stood the old man and the little boy. And right there, in the old man's hands, was her Christmas tree, and all lit up and decorated too!

"In your hurry to get home, you forgot this," said the old man. "And when my grandson came home, we decided to decorate it for you."

"It's beautiful!" said Mia. "Oh, thank you! Won't you stay for a cup of cocoa?"

"I'm afraid we don't have time," said the old man. "We still have a lot of things to do tonight. But I'm sure we'll see each other again soon." And off they went.

Mia watched as they disappeared into the snowy night. "Merry Christmas!" she called. Then, just as she was about to go inside, she noticed something odd. There were footprints in the snow behind Mopp, and footprints behind Murphy. But there were no footprints in the snow behind the old man and the little boy.

Mia smiled at Murphy and Mopp. "I think this is going to be
a very special Christmas."